By Annie Auerbach

ABDOPUBLISHING.COM

Reinforced library bound edition published in 2016 by Spotlight, a division of ABDO
PO Box 398166, Minneapolis, Minnesota 55439. Spotlight produces high-quality
reinforced library bound editions for schools and libraries. Published by agreement
with Warner Bros. Entertainment Inc.

Printed in the United States of America, North Mankato, Minnesota.
092015
012016

CATALOGING-IN-PUBLICATION DATA

Auerbach, Annie.
 Scooby-Doo in the Coolsville Contraption Contest / Annie Auerbach.
  p. cm. (Scooby-Doo)
Summary: A frightening Frankenstein monster is wrecking all of the contraptions at the Coolsville
Contraption Contest. Can Mystery, Inc. find the monster and keep the contest alive?
1. Scooby-Doo (Fictitious character)--Juvenile fiction. 2. Dogs--Juvenile fiction. 3. Mystery and
detective stories--Juvenile fiction. 4. Adventure and adventures--Juvenile fiction.
[E]--dc23
                   2015156071

978-1-61479-409-7   (Reinforced Library Bound Edition)

Spotlight

Fred had gotten a flyer in the mail. He couldn't wait to show his friends. "The annual Coolsville Contraption Contest is tonight! We have to go!" Fred exclaimed. His hobby was to build contraptions.

The whole gang piled into the Mystery Machine. They drove to the science museum, where the contest was being held.

"I can't wait to see all the cool contraptions," said Fred.

"Me, too," said Velma.

"Like, I can't wait to see if they have some cool food," said Shaggy.

"Re, roo!" added Scooby.

"Wow! Check this out!" Fred said. He pointed to a contraption that was twice as tall as he.

Just then, the contraption's creator showed up. "Hello! I'm Gerald Montgomery. Please, allow me to show you how my contraption works."

"That'd be great," Fred replied.

Mr. Montgomery dropped a metal ball down a pole. As it wound around, it set off a chain reaction. At the bottom, a spoon flipped over and began stirring a bowl of soup.

Fred and the others congratulated Mr. Montgomery. "I think you might have a chance at winning the contest."

"Oh, I hope so," he replied.

While the gang looked at the other contestants' contraptions, Velma noticed something wrong.

"Look!" said Velma. "Pieces are missing from this one."

"This one, too," Daphne said, standing in front of another one.

"Hmm," said Fred. "None of these will work if a key piece is missing."

"It's worse than that," said a voice. It belonged to Mr. Barclay, the head judge of the contest. "If a piece is missing, the whole contraption is disqualified."

"Jinkies!" said Velma.

"This has never happened before," explained Mr. Barclay. "And if we don't figure out what's going on, we'll have to cancel the contest."

"But look, not all the contraptions are missing pieces," Daphne pointed out.

"Yes," agreed the judge. "That's what's so strange."

Meanwhile, Shaggy and Scooby were busy at the refreshments stand. Inspired by the contraptions, they built their own devices to propel food into their mouths.

"Like, watch this, Scoob!" said Shaggy. He flipped a mini hot dog into his mouth with a bunch of pretzel sticks.

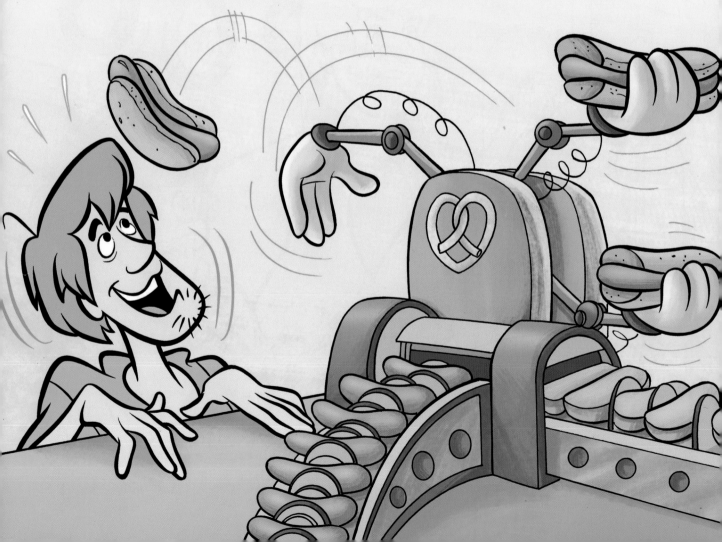

But the hot dog missed Shaggy's mouth and flew into one of the exhibit rooms. He and Scooby went after it.

Suddenly Scooby stopped. "Ruh-roh!"

Looming over him was a scary Frankenstein monster! It stretched out its arms to grab him.

"I found the hot dog!" Shaggy declared. Then he saw the monster. "Zoinks! Like, let's get out of here!"

Shaggy and Scooby ran through the exhibit hall looking for a way out.

Instead, they ran right into Fred and the others. Oof!

"There you guys are!" said Fred.

"Ruh-rye," said Scooby, waving his paw.

"Like, I'm with Scoob," said Shaggy. "Buh-bye!"

"GRRRRR!!!" grumbled the Frankenstein monster. He chased everyone out of the museum.

Out on the front steps, Fred said, "I think we have another mystery on our hands. We have to go back inside and look for clues."

"Like, I'd rather stay out here," said Shaggy. Then his stomach growled.

After Fred promised some Scooby Snacks, Shaggy and Scooby agreed to the plan.

Back inside the exhibit hall, the gang split up.

Shaggy and Scooby searched behind and under the refreshments table.

"Like, this doesn't look like food," said Shaggy. He held up a metal bolt between two fingers.

"Reah," agreed Scooby.

Fred, Velma, and Daphne noticed that more of the contestants' contraptions were missing pieces. One contraption was completely dismantled. It sat in a heap on the floor.

"We better find out who's behind this before all the contraptions are destroyed!" said Daphne.

"Look at this!" Velma called.

Fred and Daphne rushed over to see what Velma had found:

makeup on a piece of a contraption.

Just then, Shaggy and Scooby raced over. "Look what we found," said Shaggy. He showed the others the bolt he found under the table.

"Jeepers," said Daphne. "You think the Frankenstein monster is behind the contraption sabotage?"

"I'm not sure," said Fred. "But we're going to find out. Come on, I've got a plan!"

Fred led everyone out to the Mystery Machine. He told the others to grab things out of the van like crates, strings, and more. When they reentered the museum, Fred got permission from the other contestants to use some of the pieces from the broken contraptions.

"We're going to build a Mega Trap to capture that monster," Fred explained.

While Shaggy and Scooby kept watch, Velma and Daphne helped Fred put together his own original contraption.

When the Mega Trap was finished, Fred said, "Shaggy and Scooby, I need you to stand guard. I'm hoping since it hasn't been broken yet, the monster will come after it next."

The pair wasn't happy about being the bait in the plan, but with the promise of some Scooby Snacks, they agreed.

"Like, here monster, monster," called Shaggy. "Here's a nice assembled contraption for you!"

"Rome and ret it!" said Scooby.

Sure enough, the Frankenstein monster lumbered down the hall toward them.

"Zoinks!" cried Shaggy. "Like, run, Scoob!"

Just as Fred hoped, the monster came after Fred's Mega Trap.
Whoosh! Ka-pow! Snap! BAM! The monster was trapped!
"Gotcha!" Fred cried.

The gang quickly tied up the monster.

"I can't wait to see who's behind this mess," said Mr. Barclay.

"Let's find out," Fred said and pulled off the monster's mask.

"Gerald Montgomery!" exclaimed Mr. Barclay. "You caused all this? But why?"

"I wanted to win the contest!" said Mr. Montgomery. "And I would have gotten away with it if it wasn't for you meddling kids and your dog!"

"But, like, why dress up as a monster?" asked Shaggy.

"I think I know why," said Velma. "He didn't have enough time to destroy the other contraptions, so he had to think of a way to get us out of the museum before the judging was complete."

"Well, I think I can say that the judging is now complete," said Mr. Barclay. "And Fred, you and your friends have won Best In Show for your Mega Trap contraption!"

"Roo-ray!" cheered Scooby-Doo.